Sniffing for Democracy

Written and Illustrated

By

Nora P. Meek

"Fly Weed to the Moon" was based on "Fly Bush to the Moon" reprinted in part with permission of Annie Fonda, author. "Fly Bush to the Moon" was recorded by Peace de Resistance. The original song "Fly Me to the Moon" was written by Howard Bart.

Sniffing for Democracy is based on a story idea by Pamela Meek.

ISBN 0-9753852-0-8

Printed in the U.S.A.

For Rêve
My God spelled backwards

Contents

Chapter 1
Freedom of Speech Takes a Dive

It all started in Massachusetts. Bassettown, Massachusetts, to be exact. Hello, my name is Spangle, and I'd like to tell you my story. It began as I waltzed out of my apartment, wearing my favorite hat. My hat just *happened* to say "Mow down the Weed" because I *happened* to be a Pawcrat and our president Fred Weed, just *happened* to be a Puglian. I thought it *happened* to be a very nice hat that expressed *my* opinion.

No sooner did I get out of the building than three dogs leapt out of nowhere, handcuffed me and pressed me against my newly polished car.

"Mmphh!" I cried, muffled by my own windshield.

"Shaddap!" yelled the dog that pinned me down. He had on a top hat and really needed a dentist appointment.

The two snickering fellows behind me just grinned. One of them had a long nose and was very slim and tall with a bandage around his tail. The other was a tiny little guy with one single diamond-shaped stripe down his back.

"Who are you?" I asked.

"I'm Jagg," said the dog with the top hat.

"Wrap," said the skinny dog in the back.

"And Pinch!" chimed in the third little dog. "And together, we're the Puglians!"

Jagg finally loosened his grip on me. "You're going with us," he said, saying it like it was a fact.

"What? Why!?!" I demanded.

Wrap motioned to my hat.

"What are you guys, some kind of fashion police?" I snapped smartly. It was no secret that I didn't like Fred Weed. Why, he wasn't even a dog! But to be arrested for wearing a hat?!

Jagg just scowled and shoved me into a shabby van. We sped off down the street, finally stopping at the local.....POUND!!!! They jerked me into a cell and closed the barred door. They left shutting the door to freedom behind them.

"Another one bites the dust," said a croaky voice.

"Wh-wh-who's there?" I asked.

"Over here, kid."

Chapter 2
Spangle Saves the Day

I turned, peering through the iron bars to discover a golden retriever. He wasn't exactly golden, his fur was tattered, and it was a rusty, yellow-bronze color.

"What do you mean by that? What's your name? Where do you get off?" I asked.

"Whoa there, cowdog!" he said. "Not too many questions. I mean, you're the eleventh dog to be put here for being anti-Weed."

I looked around to the other barred stalls. I saw about eleven dogs in all, including me and the dog next to me.

"My name is Butch. Yours?"

Nervous, I hesitated. I finally said, "M-my name's Spangle."

He didn't really listen to me, and instead went on to another question. "You got sharp claws?" he asked.

I thought that was a very awkward question to ask, judging by the place we were in. "Yeah, I guess so..." I replied to Butch, lifting my right paw up and examining it.

"Good," he grunted and slid a big bone that had many scratches and bite marks on it between the bars of my cell. I tried to lift it up, but it weighed a ton!

"What's this thing made out of, lead?" I exclaimed.

"You never mind what it's made out of," Butch snapped. "All you have to do is chew it and claw it in the shape of that keyhole there." He pointed to the keyhole on my cell door.

I frowned. How was I going to make a key out of a chrome bone? I started gnawing at it and scratching it. Three hours later it was the perfect shape and size to fit into the keyhole. I slid it back over to Butch when I was finished.

"Doggone great!" he cried when he saw it, as if I had rescued a giraffe from a raging fire. He picked the bone up with one paw. What??? He could lift that thing with ease! Anyway, Butch slipped it into the keyhole of the lock, turned it a couple of times and his cage door creaked open. He walked over to my door and opened it, as well as everyone else's.

Butch and I crept to the exit door with the nine other dogs trailing behind. A dog who was obviously supposed to be guarding the exit was hunched over a desk face down asleep in his own drool. We silently tiptoed passed him and flung the door open to a beautiful sun-filled day outside. All the dogs except Butch ran outside and bounded home.

Butch stopped me before I could go back to my house. "I just wanted to thank you," he said, "for all that you've done for us. Nobody else could make that bone a key. They broke all their teeth and scratched their claws trying; but, you made that key for us, Spangle, and I want you to have this in your journeys."

He handed me a bronze compass on a gold chain. It was kind of odd. I asked, "Why are you giving me this?"

"Trust me," he said. "You'll need it." and he walked off.

I put the compass in my pocket and went home.

A couple of days later I wrote a letter to the editor of the Bassettown Post, complaining about what had happened to me.

October 5, 2003

Dear Dog Post,

My name is Spangle Wagger. I'm writing you to inform you about what happened to me August 24, 2003. As I was waltzing out of my house three dogs, also known as the Puglians, handcuffed me and took me to the pound. Why? Because I was wearing a hat that said, "Mow down the Weed." I think it's my right to express what I feel about the president, Fred Weed. They took me to the pound and luckily I got out using the right equipment and freed the other dogs impounded for the same thing. I would like you to publish a story about this so other dogs can know how wrong it is to dismiss free speech. Wake up and smell the stench!

Sincerely,

Spangle Wagger

I waited and waited for the Post to write a story about this infringement on the rights of dogs in Bassettown. In fact, I was thinking about it again when I heard a rapping on my door. I peered through the peephole and saw the Puglians.

"Come out!" yelled Jagg. "We know you sent that article to the Bassettown Post! The article and your hat were insults to the president. We're taking you back to the pound!"

Without thinking, I ran out my back door, got into my Spotted Urban Vehicle, or SUV, and sped off. "This is the last straw," I said to myself. "Not only were the Pugs trying to get me to stop wearing my hat, the Post wouldn't investigate my story. They turned me over to the Pugs. What was this country coming to? Soon they'll be telling me what to think!" I stepped on the gas pedal. Out loud I said, "This democracy doesn't smell right. I'm gonna find one that does or die trying! I hope it's the first one!"

Chapter 3
A Surprise Discovery in Raw Hyde Park

I caught the first plane out of Bassettown International Airport. It happened to be going to London, England. I had heard of that place. They had a town square where dogs gathered and listened to other dogs expound on whatever they were thinking. Good. I needed a dose of unfiltered free speech!

I found Raw Hyde Square easily. Just as I'd heard, there was a dog standing on a box talking about something. As I got closer I realized he was talking about the mess in the United States of Dogs.

"Gentledogs, I come here to talk about our friends across the pond, the U.S. of D. I'm troubled by what I'm hearing about the way things are going there. Fred Weed, the President, refuses to sign on to the Boneyoto treaty which helps the world stop global warming. We all know that's bad for dogs. Smell the air. It gets more bitter everyday. Look at those cars they use. They pollute the air dogs breathe all over the world. They don't even know about the Puppy T Cruisers that we drive in London which don't pollute. Why the Cruisers are even made in our country by a company from the U.S.D.--Damzel-Chihauhau! Shocking. Truly shocking.

I couldn't believe my ears. I'd never heard of these Puppy T Cruisers. I set out to find one right away.

I found the nearest Puppy T Cruiser dealer and here's what I found out. It was small, only 2.5 meters long, had only 2 seats, and had lower CO_2 emissions than any other car. What? Lower CO_2 emissions meant it cost less to drive and it protected the air. Wow! 58.9 miles per gallon. Why my SUV only gets 15 miles per gallon. Boy, did I feel guilty driving that thing!

I rented a cruiser and drove to France.

Chapter 4
Spangle Meets Liberté

I crossed the Channel on a ferry and drove straight to Paris, the capitol of France. I stayed at the Hotel de les Rêves, which meant Hotel of Dreams. I decided I'd go around and poll everybody to see how the democracy was there.

I started out with the mansion next door. I knocked on the front door and a very beautiful and oddly colored pinkish dog stepped out. "Bonjour," she said.

This was gonna be hard as I thought she spoke French, and only French. I hesitated and said the one sentence I knew in French. "Parlais vous Englais?" I asked her.

She giggled and said, "Yes, sir."

I sighed with relief. Then I told her, "I'm polling everyone I meet in France to see if the democracy smells any good here. I come from the U. S. of D. where Fred Weed is our president. That's why I'm here. I want to know if I could live in France, but only if the aroma's right. Do you get my drift?"

She smiled "I know of zees Fred Weed. He's never been here, but I 'ave read newspapers and I know zat 'e haz never been anywhere before 'e vas zelected as president."

I laughed. Yeah, that was our Fred Weed.

"Plus," she said, "He'z a monkey!" She shook her head in despair. "Mon Dieu. Zose monkeyz sink zey are better zan us."

"Yes, he doesn't have compassion for the common dog. Hey, what's your name?"

"My name iz Liberté. Zis means liberty in Englais."

"My name is Spangle," I told her.

"Well, Spangle," Liberté said, "All I know iz...I do not like zis Weed. 'E tells dogs not to eat French Fries because 'e iz angry at us. And, Spangle, he does not even know the French did not invent zee French Fry!"

"Really. Who did?"

"Ze Belgians made zem first."

"Mow down the Weed, is what I say. But, how is your democracy?"

"Well, I zink it's a little zmelly like yours. I sink you need to zearch for a better one zan zis one."

Oh," I said, "Do you recommend any places?" I asked.

"Oui!" she exclaimed. "Zey started a new democracy in Russia. Maybe zat's a good place to start. May I go with you?"

"Sure!" I said without thinking, "But, why?"

"I'd love to zmell zee zcent of a good democracy!"

Chapter 5
What Does Capitalism Smell Like?

During the plane ride Liberté told me about Russia. "Russia'z a good place to go, you zee, zey uzed to 'ave zee communizm, but zey had zat revolution. Zey now 'ave a democracy. We should be able to zmell if it'z good enough for us without asking around."

"I hope so," I murmured.

When we got to Moscow a Russian walked up to us on the street. He had a stern look on his face, a big hat on his head and a fuzzy coat over his brown fur. He sure was big!

"Hello," he said, in a big loud voice.

I felt like I was shrinking by the second, that guy was so big.

"What are your names?" he boomed.

"Spangle," I said reluctantly.

Liberté didn't seem to notice how gargantuan he was and opened up to him right away. "My name iz Liberté. What is your name, zir?

"My name," he snapped, "is Gorbachok."

Liberté and I snickered. He sounded like something you'd eat for dinner. I tried to hold in a comment but it just came out. "Can I call you Gorby?" I giggled.

His face got red with fury. It looked like he was about to blow a gasket! I guess Gorbachok was kinda sensitive.

He finally calmed himself down. Liberté tried to go onto another subject, and asked the question we both came there for.

"Monsieur," she said. "May I ask a question?"

"You just did!" he shouted.

"No, no, no," she replied. "I want to know vat zee government iz like here, you know? Avter you 'ad zat revolution and all."

"Oh yes, that." He said, lowering his voice to a normal tone, "We can buy any bones and steaks we like but we can't bark about everything we want to."

"That reeks," said Liberté as she exchanged a knowing look with me.

I shrugged. "Well, Gorbachok," I said, "got to go."

Liberté and I headed over to the nearest airport.

On the way Liberté had an idea. "I've alwayz wanted to visit China. I hear zey have a beeg wall zere."

"Let's go!" I said.

Chapter 6
Up Against the Great Wall of Outsourcing

In China we hired a tour guide to lead us around during our stay. His name was Lingfu. He had his ears pinned back with what looked like black chop sticks, and was wearing a red and gold robe with a dragon embroidered on it. We never asked why.

He showed us all the sights and sounds of China, then I finally asked him what I was really there for. "Lingfu," I said, "is the democracy good here?"

Lingfu turned around slowly. "Here, in China," he said, as he lowered his voice and placed his paws inside the sleeves of his robe, "we have no democracy. All is dictatorship. We look to you for answers," and bowed his head. He did that often.

"What do you like about the United States of Dogs?"

"Many dogs from China traveled to United States because they heard that the streets there were paved with gold. If you work good job there you get lots and lots of money, and you have one ruler every four years, not for a lifetime."

Liberté and I just shook our heads. We knew that he was talking about capitalism, not democracy. Besides all our jobs were going to his country. We hated to break it to him, so we didn't say much more, just that we were going someplace else—Australia.

Chapter 7
Every Vote Doesn't Count Down Under

It took us a long time, but we finally got to Australia. We were on a private tour bus with another tour guide; her name was Sheila.

She and Liberté became fast friends. They were busy talking; but, I decided to nose in with my question. I couldn't wait all day.

"Sheila," I said, "how's the democracy down under?" She turned from Liberté. "Oi mate!" she replied, "to put it in a way, it's democracy for some, but not for all!"

"What do you mean, Sheila?" I questioned.

"Well, there's the problem of the original dogs, the aborigines; I'm one of 'em. I don't 'ave no rights, I don't. I can work but I can't vote. It's downright, it's downright undemocratic, mate. We was the first one's 'ere, we was. It's our country. Why don't they just leave us alone? Anyway, enough 'bout me. Why do you ask such a question, mate?"

"I'm sniffing all over the globe for the right democracy. I left Bassettown, Massachusetts over a month ago. I met Liberté in Paris and she decided to join me."

"Well, you're on the wrong track if you're trying to live here, mate. This democracy has a horrible smell. I know that as a tour guide I'm supposed to attract dogs to this island, but honesty is the best policy, ya know."

Liberté and I thanked her for all the advice, but we still had one more problem. "Sheila, where do you suppose we go next?" I asked.

"I suggest ya go to South Africa, it's a fun place, and they just started a new democracy."

And, with that, we both left for the Australian cruise ship, Boomerang, compliments of Sheila herself.

Chapter 8
The Writing's on the Cave Wall

The cruise took 2 weeks! But we enjoyed the sun and the 24/7 buffets filled with beef chunks, peanut butter and bones. One day out by the pool we overheard a newscast by the Canine News Network.

> ...and we understand that President Weed has locked up several dogs in Minnesota for protesting his government...60 scientists complain that Weed won't let their research guide decisions for dog safety and health...Weed's business buddies get to keep all the money they stole from dogs...obedience schools won't get the money they were promised...

Soon after we reached Cape Town we met an English-speaking native; his name was Lickick. He wore a brightly patterned tarp and a bandanna over his head. He gave us a rundown of the many places that we could explore from caves to waterfalls.

We decided to visit the caves where he said the first dogs lived. When we got there, we saw many cave paintings of dogs hunting, barking and dancing. Lickick knew how to read the cave drawings. They told stories. The stories were from before our time; they were from the first of all times. Lickick read us one of them:

> The Woman greets the Man. "Good morning, did you sleep well?" The Man says, "I slept well, if you slept well."

"Huh?" I was confused.

"That's Ubonetu," said Lickick. "We believe in Ubonetu in Africa."

"What's that?" asked Liberté.

"Well, ma'am it's like if Spangle bites you, he hurts you and he hurts himself. If he helps you, he helps himself. We are all connected."

As Lickick was speaking I decided to butt in. "Is that democracy?" I asked.

Lickick paused for a second. "Yes. We believe that if something hurts the common dog it is not good even if it saves money."

"So you've got a right smelling democracy here!"

"No, not yet. We're in a bit of chaos you see. We have been ruled by monkeys for a long time and we are trying to go back to what our ancestors taught us."

We kept walking on deeper into the cave. Deeper. Deeper. It got more and more dark. I could see Liberté next to me, but I wanted to ask Lickick a question about the cave painting we had passed a second ago. It was an arrow pointing forward. But Lickick wasn't where he was supposed to be. In fact, he wasn't anywhere. It was just Liberté and me.

Liberté didn't seem to notice, so I played it cool. We kept on walking into the darkness. Pitch-black darkness. Suddenly we both stepped onto a cushion like material. The floor wasn't hard stone anymore. It felt just like a mattress. Then I saw blue and yellow sparks everywhere. Suddenly, it was light out again and we were out of the cave. Only...we weren't in Africa anymore.

Chapter 9
Back to the Past

We were in a theme park! There were lots of dogs walking around in old-time clothing. In the distance was the Liberty Belle. But...something felt funny.

"Where are we?" I said to Liberté.

"Let'z go over to zat tailor shop and ask zomeone zere."

We went inside and there was a dog sitting in a chair wearing old-time clothing with fabric in her lap. She looked frustrated.

I walked over to her.

"Hi, I'm Spangle," I said to her.

She said as she looked up "Hello, I'm Betsy. Betsy Ross."

I paused for a minute. That name struck a bell in my head but I couldn't quite put my paw on it. I searched my memory and said, "I'm afraid we're lost. Can you tell me where we are?"

Betsy smiled "Why you're in Philadelphia."

"OK," I said. "Are we in a theme park? Dogs here dress funny."

Betsy's smile disappeared. "What's a theme park?" she asked. "Dogs in Philadelphia don't dress funny. This is the casual wear of today, the modern world."

"Modern? What year is this?" I demanded.

"Why, Spangle, it's the year 1776 in the month of May."

I took a step backwards. "Er, we'll just leave now."

"Wait," she said.

"Your fur. It sparks an idea in my mind. I'm trying to make a new flag to represent our 13 colonies. Red and white stripes are ok, but blue and white stars are perfect to represent the colonies. Hold still Spangle."

She took out a piece of parchment and began to sketch something. It was a picture of a United States of Dogs flag in its early stages with a circle of white stars in a blue square with red and white stripes everywhere else.

Now I remembered who Betsy Ross was. She created the first flag for our country!

"Thank you for the idea, Spangle. You can leave now if you like."

"OK," I said. As we left I noticed Betsy cutting out a 5-pointed star in a single snip. Now that was cool! No wonder they chose her to make the flag.

Out on the street we didn't quite know what to do. We looked in lots of store fronts to try to figure things out. Soon we came upon a sign for a shop that said "Franklin's Print Shop."

Chapter 10
What is Democracy?

We looked in the door and saw a dog with golden fur and very long ears drooping down at the sides of his head. I recognized him as Ben Franklin.

"Mr. Franklin," I said rushing up to him, "It's great to meet you!"

Ben Franklin looked at me funny. "Excuse me, have I met you before, sir?" he asked.

"Oh," I remembered. I'd read about him in lots of history books but he'd never heard of me.

"Mr. Franklin, my name is Spangle and this is my friend, Liberté."

"Nice to meet you, Spangle and Liberté."

"We've heard all about you."

Ben frowned. "But I'm not famous. At least not yet." He walked around his print shop looking at papers as he spoke. "Tomorrow I'll go outside in stormy weather with a key attached to the end of a kite. This is one of my experiments. I'm very excited to see how it'll turn out."

I sighed because I knew what was going to happen. But I didn't tell him. That would spoil his fun.

"May I ask why you are here?" he questioned as he walked over to Liberté.

Before I could answer Liberté spoke up for the first time since coming to Philadelphia. "Ve're zearching throughout ze vorld vor a good democracy."

"Oh," exclaimed Ben, "We're working on just the same thing. Perhaps we can help each other!"

"What do you mean?" I asked.

He took us around his print shop and explained what he meant. "You see the reason I started this print shop is to spread news quickly to commoners. A newspaper spreads democracy faster."

Liberté jumped up. "I remember zat. My grandmozer told me about vat you did ven I waz young. She zaid you vere a good man."

Ben stopped at her last words and stared at her. "Were?" he said.

Liberté hesitated. "I meant...are."

We heard a knock at the door. Scared, we held our breaths. Who was that?

"Thomas! Welcome, you're just in time! I have some visitors who are asking about democracy and whether we have one here. What do you say to that?"

Tom said, "Hello, my name's Tom Paine. I wrote something called Common Sense back in January. I was sick of the English King trying to tell us what to do. Would you like a copy?"

"Uh...you wrote Common Sense? You're Thomas Paine? How do you do sir!?" I asked.

Ben added "Turns out lots of us are sick of the King. Tom's book started a revolution. We're in the midst of it now. Tom Jefferson is on his way here to help write our Declaration of Independence."

My mouth dropped and some drool slipped out. Ben noticed.

"Anyway...we know a lot about politics, government and the right democracy if you ever need any advice."

"Yeah, lay it on us!" I said.

Tom Paine started. "Well, you know, these are the times that try dog's souls. We live in a time when the common dog has no say over his life."

"Kinda like uz," said Liberté as she poked me.

"Dogs know how to smell when something's right. A King can't know what's right for us. He's never had to smell. Only we do!" continued Tom. "It's only common sense that dogs should choose who rules them."

Ben added, "But dogs should not be ruled. Dogs should choose the ruler and determine how the ruler shall lead."

"Yes, just because someone is wealthy or has inherited a birthright doesn't mean they shall be the ruler. All voices are equal. A mutt is equal to a pedigreed dog. Money shouldn't determine what the rules are. The common dog should determine what's best."

"Ok," said Liberté, "but the final test iz ze zmell. What does a right democracy zmell like to you?"

"Exhilarating," said Tom matter of factly.

Ben turned to us, "What's it like where you come from? Where do you come from anyway?"

Uh, oh. Now what to do. I didn't know whether to tell him what was to come in the future or make up a story. All of a sudden Liberté and I were surrounded by blue and yellow sparks popping and poof we were outta there.

Chapter 11
Mow Down the Trees or Mow Down the Weed?

I didn't know where we were, but I knew one thing, I was freezing.

"Where do you think we are now?" I asked Liberté.

"Vat year is it?" she replied.

We were on the outskirts of some town in a really cold place. We kept walking toward the lights in the distance. It was a small town. That's for sure. We found a discount clothing store and went in to look for some warm clothes. The name of the shop was Alaskan Clothes for Dogs.

Liberté whispered "We must be in Alaska!"

"Let's find parkas, then, ask the clerk what day it is," I said.

We found some parkas and took them up to the cashier. "Just curious, sir, do you happen to know what day it is?" I asked.

He looked at me kind of funny. "Why, it's Saturday," he said.

"Uh, no, I mean the actual date," I said sheepishly.

"Okay...it's February 4th."

"Okay...and the year?"

His ears perked way up on that one. "2004," he said. "Where you been, buddy?"

"That's a long story and I don't have time. Just let me buy those parkas and we've got to be going. Oh...one more thing...where exactly are we?"

He was used to me by now, so he just said "Akitaland, Alaska."

We hurried out of the store. "My friends, Belle and Koopa, live in Akitaland. Let's find them."

"How?" Liberté asked.

"I know. We'll put my compass to use! She lives 2 miles east of Akitaland. Wonder what it smells like at their place." I quickly took my compass out of my pocket.

I found east on the compass and we started our trek. We trudged through a blizzard for what seemed like hours because we were so cold. We found out that we needed about a thousand of the parka's to keep us warm. Then, through the blizzard I saw two spots on the horizon. I realized it was my friends, Belle and Koopa. As we approached an unpleasant odor wafted from the trees.

When we got up to them I saw that they were wearing seal skin mittens, caribou fur coats and ptarmigan shoes. Ptarmigan's the chicken of the north. They held out fresh whale blubber but we politely refused. After that they took me inside their igloo. Bell started making a fire while she talked. She was my friend first and had introduced me to her husband Koopa.

Belle said, "I'm sorry we aren't able to offer you more than whale blubber. We're scarce on food."

Koopa grunted. "Yes," he said, "ever since those lumberjacks came and chopped down so many trees in our forest, we've had trouble finding food."

Belle continued where Koopa left off. "They destroyed homes for the animals we hunt and polluted the water where the fish we eat reside." The igloo fell silent for a moment.

Then, I said in a quiet voice, "I recognize that smell now. Fred Weed let them cut down the forest."

Belle gasped. "Weed?"

"That's why I say 'Mow down Weed, not trees!'"

Silence. "Well, I'm not surprised," she said finally. "He likes to pretend he's one of us, but we know he's not. A monkey is not a dog."

Liberté spoke up, "Belle, Koopa and Zpangle...I 'ave a zuggestion."

"What?" they asked.

"Let'z get a bus and gathzer up as many dogz as ve can and take ze country back from Fred Veed!"

"Whoa there," I said. "That's a big job."

"You can do eet...you 'ave to," said Liberté, "and zee French need you to az vell."

"You're right. I know. Let's go see Cousin Banner in Kansas and see if he wants to join us!"

Chapter 12
Take a Whiff of This!

We climbed in Belle and Koopa's old van and headed for Kansas. We decided to visit my Cousin, Banner, a farmer in Kansas. Perhaps a trip to the heartland would cheer us up.

On the way we picked up a Bassettown Post at a gas station. The headline read: "Weed Starts Fight with Bully Rott." Bully Rott was a guy who was half Bull Dog and half Rottweiler. He was also in charge of a country half-way around the world filled with other Bully Rotters. Chow-Chow, Weed's vice-president, was in on it, too.

"Why'd Weed and Chow-Chow do that?" asked Belle. "Bully Rott wasn't doing anything to us!"

"Yeah, I heard of Bully Rott. He was a bad guy, but he hadn't threatened the U.S. of Dogs...I thought we were supposed to wait for someone to attack us. Aren't peaceful dogs supposed to keep their heads down unless...." Koopa said.

I added, "...unless another dog comes into their territory..."

"...een a ferocious vay," finished Liberté.

A pall settled over the bus. News of Weed's fight half-way around the world was not good. We thought amongst ourselves. We slept, chewed bones and listened to our favorite singer, Frank Schnauzer on the CD player. After we heard him sing "Fly Me to the Moon" Belle jumped up and said "Hold on to your tails, doggies. Frank just inspired me." She stood up in the aisle and sang:

Fly Weed to the moon and let him play among the stars
Let him see what spring is like on Jupiter and Mars
In other words, go away
In other words, we won't miss you

You'll be happy out in space
You'll feel the King of all you see
You won't have to deal with dogs who insist on being free
And when you go... take Chowney
And leave the Earth safe for peace.

You can be our star wars spinning high above the Earth
You won't be here to see our transformation and rebirth
In other words, hit the road
In other words, don't come back here

Floating out in space you'll see the Earth and all her grace
Perhaps you'll start to grasp the oneness of the canine race
Until you do, stay above, and leave the Earth safe for love.

When we arrived we found Cousin Banner spraying his wheat harvest with a can of pesticide. He saw us and waved looking like the American flag rippling in the breeze.

"Hi, Cousin Banner," I said. He turned his red and white head to me and lifted his straw hat off his head to get a better view. He squinted at me for a while and finally recognized me.

"Howdy, Cousin Spangle," he said. "What are y'all doing in this here part o' Kansas?"

"Well, I'll tell you. We're searching the U.S.D. to find a right democracy."

Cousin Banner scratched his head. "Well, I suppose we have one of those in the shed."

I shook my head. "No, no, it's complicated." I looked down at his can of pesticide. "I see you're spraying your crops."

"Yes," Cousin Banner sighed. "But, I don't know why. I get more crops but they're not as healthy as they used to be. The pesticide gets in lots o' dogs' blood and makes 'em sick."

"Why don't you just sue the pesticide makers?"

"Nope," Cousin Banner replied. "Already tried that."

"What happened?"

"All they did was tell me I had no right to get money from 'em."

"You mean they said you didn't have the right to sue them?"

"Yup, that's pretty much it. I don't bother with those business folks no more. They just care about making money. They don't care about the health o' dogs."

"Well,' I mumbled to myself, "that's another reason to mow down that Weed. First the trees and now this."

"What'd you say?"

"Cousin Banner, we're on a mission. Do you want to join us? We're looking for dogs who can put their noses to good use."

Banner joined us in the van. As he walked down the aisle he slapped paws with Koopa, Belle, and Liberté.

"You know," said Banner, "Florida's great this time of year. Plus, Allie's there."

I perked up, remembering Allie.

Chapter 13
Talk About Stench! Florida

Our journey to Florida was fun. We picked up some bones at a dogateria and wiled away the time chewing. We chewed so much we even started making music with our chews. Koopa whistled while he chewed, Belle did a little percussion, and I played bass.

I grew up in Florida so I was curious to go back to my roots. The Everglades was one of my favorite places. Now that's a place to get a whiff of nature.

My old friend, Allie, the Alligator had lived there for 50 years. She lived in some tall grasses on the edge of the Everglades near Komondor. No sooner had we gotten there than we noticed a pungent smell.

"Whew!" said Belle. "Get a whiff of that! I've never sniffed anything like it!"

"Me neither," said Cousin Banner.

"I wonder vat it iz?" Liberté thought aloud.

I figured we'd ask Allie when we found her.

I led the way and walked to a tall clump of grass. The others followed close behind.

I heard some rustling. "Allie," I called. "Allie...it's me, your old friend, Spangle."

"Spangle!" I heard her say. "Long time no see? What're you here for?"

"That's a long story."

"How ya been doin'?"

"Well, not so good. I was arrested back home in Bassettown for saying something against the Weed. I escaped and started traveling trying to find a democracy that smelled right. But everywhere I go it stinks!"

A disgruntled Allie said "Yeah, can you smell the stench here?"

"We were gonna mention that. Oh, yeah, meet my friends." I introduced everyone.

"What's that dern smell?" asked Cousin Banner.

"Weed's folks decided that polluters could keep on polluting, especially with something called phosphorus. Don't ask me what that is. But your nose knows!"

"Speaking about a disgusting odor, Allie, have you guys in Florida ever recovered from that election?"

"No, not really. The black and chocolate labs are still upset. They weren't allowed to vote. And those old dogs in Paw Beach got confused and put their paws on Weed's name by mistake..."

"What's a right democracy without a vote?" said Koopa.

"You know what I suggest?" Belle asked.

"What?"

"You run for president, Spangle!" Belle shouted.

"Spangle for President!" they all shouted.

Liberté chimed in "Zpangle, remember vat we learned from Tom and Ben."

"What was that?" I asked.

"Democracy ztarts vith ze common dog. Zat meanz uz. You've got to truzt your nozez and get ze United Ztates of Dogz back on zee right path!"

"That's it!" I shouted. "We'll start a new movement... and call it...Sniffing for Democracy!'"

The sun was going down in the Everglades. The sky was a pink crimson. We made a fire, cooked some chili-bone soup and settled in to sleep.

In the morning I woke up to find the others decorating the van. "Sniffing for Democracy" was written in large letters along the sides. Across the front and back they had written "Spangle for President!"

Chapter 14
Election 2004!

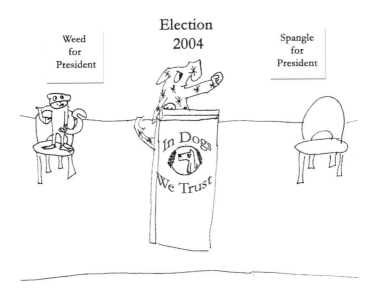

The night before the election Weed and I gave speeches at a town hall in Washington, DC. Liberté, Koopa, Belle and Cousin Banner sat in the front row. It was great to see them. As I looked around I saw hundreds of signs saying "Dogs for Truth," "Trust your Nose" and, of course, "Sniffing for Democracy."

We both gave our speeches and the dogs clapped more for me than for Weed, mainly because my speech was better....It was just off of the top of my head, but Weed's speech was a bunch of hoots and hollers. I thought monkeys were smarter than that!

I said, "It's very simple, Doggies! Weed's way doesn't smell right. The water stinks, the dirt's poisoned, and the air reeks. We need to take care of the Earth. She's the only one we've got! We need to start a Department of Peace. Biting is NOT ok! To harm another is to wound one's soul. We need to take care of the dogs in the United States and the Dogs of the world. Does it make sense to have a monkey in charge when dogs are the ones who are sensible? To sense is to smell and that's what dogs are good at. We have no choice but to throw Weed out. Let's trust our noses. I'd be honored to help the common dog in all of us unearth a democracy that smells right."

The audience clapped their paws and cheered.

The Next Day

"I'm president?" I asked myself. That was great. I was elected president of the United States of Dogs. I sniffed the air. It smelled better already. Ahhh....Ben and Tom were right. The aroma was invigorating. I had finally, after sniffing all over the world, found true democracy right under my nose. I tipped my cap to Tom and Ben, and sat down. It had been a long journey.

The End

Suggested Reading

Thomas Paine. Common Sense, 1776

For information about Ubuntu:
Ubuntu and Cultural Revival by Edwin Pillay published by sadtu.org

Terrorists and Saints: The Wisdom of Ubuntu by Eric Sirotkin published by Sentient Times

Life in Full colour: Ubuntu by Simon Goland published by simongoland.com

Ubuntu: An African Assessment of the Religious Other by Dirk J. Louw, University of the North

For information on the Environment

National Resources Defense Council

Republicons.org

www.aclunc.org/911 American Civil Liberties Union

The Constitution of the United States of America

www.thesmart.co.uk The Smart Car

Questions and Topics for Discussion

1. In Chapter 1 Spangle is arrested for criticizing the president. Is appropriate in a democracy? Why or why not?

2. The president's name is Weed. How do you think Ms Meek came up with that for the president's name? Can you think of a some other names for the president?

3. In Chapter 3 the speaker in Raw Hyde Park talks about the Boneyoto Treaty. This was a take off on the Kyoto Treaty. What is the Kyoto Treaty and how do you think the United States should respond to it?

4. The main character in Chapter 5 is named Gorbachok. Who do you think this refers to and what were some of his accomplishments?

5. What is outsourcing? How do you think this fits in with the global economy? Is it good for the United States?

6. Chapter 7 talks about the aborigines in Australia. What is the history of the aborigines? What similarities do you see in the history of the United States?

7. Ubonetu in Chapter 8 refers to the African concept of Ubuntu. Compare Ubuntu to democracy.

8. Who was Thomas Paine and what did he contribute to democracy in the United States?

9. How do you feel about deforestation and its effects on the environment?

10. What happened in Florida during Election 2000?

11. What kind of president do you think Spangle will be? What do you think his guiding principles will be?

About the Author

Nora P. Meek, age 11, loves dogs and dedicates this book to Rêve, her beloved Labrador Retriever who died this year. Nora lives with her parents and is an avid reader and writer. She also loves drawing and making sculptures and has shown her artwork in venues from Washington, DC to Baltimore, New Orleans and Miami.

6645349R0